Magic
Animal Friends

For Maisie Nolan
in Manchester

Special thanks to Valerie Wilding

ISBN 978-0-545-90747-7

Text copyright © 2015 by Working Partners Limited
Illustrations © 2015 by Working Partners Limited

Series author: Daisy Meadows

All rights reserved. Published by Scholastic Inc., *Publishers since 1920*,
by arrangement with Working Partners Limited. Series created
by Working Partners Limited, London.

SCHOLASTIC and associated logos are trademarks and/or
registered trademarks of Scholastic Inc. MAGIC ANIMAL FRIENDS
is a trademark of Working Partners Limited.

10 9 8 7 6 5 4 3 2 1   16 17 18 19 20

Printed in the U.S.A.   40
First printing 2016

Rosie Gigglepip's Lucky Escape

Daisy Meadows

Scholastic Inc.

Shining House

Sunshine Meadow

Blossom Briar

Toadstool Café

Goldie's Grotto

Toadstool Glade

Mrs. Taptree's Library

Friendship Tree

Maze

Silver Spring

Buttercup Grove

Lighthouse

Can you keep a secret? I thought you could!

Then I'll tell you about an enchanted wood.

It lies through the door in the old oak tree.

Let's go there now—just follow me!

We'll find adventure that never ends,

And meet the Magic Animal Friends!

Love,
Goldie the Cat

Contents

CHAPTER ONE

A Visit from Goldie

Lily Hart cradled a guinea pig in her arms as she waited at the barn door for her best friend. The tiny animal peeped happily as Lily gently pet its chocolate-brown fur.

"You're almost asleep, Coco!" Lily said as the guinea pig's eyes began to close.

The barn was hidden behind a group of trees in Lily's yard. Mr. and Mrs. Hart had converted it into the Helping Paw Wildlife Hospital, and all kinds of animals were taken care of there. Both Lily and her friend Jess adored animals and loved to help out whenever they could!

Suddenly Lily saw a girl with blond curly hair and a big grin running toward her. Jess! In moments, Jess was petting the guinea pig delightedly.

"Coco's leg healed quickly, didn't it?" Jess said happily.

Lily nodded. "But she still seems not quite herself. She's always so sleepy."

They went into the barn, which was filled with hutches of all shapes and sizes. Jess opened the door of an empty hutch, and Lily gently put Coco inside.

The guinea pig squeaked noisily as she

crept into a corner and settled into the fresh sawdust.

Lily sighed. "I'm sure there's something else wrong with her. I wish I knew what. Mom and Dad don't know, either."

"And they know everything there is to know about animals," said Jess. Mr. and Mrs. Hart were both vets. "Maybe she's missing her owner," she suggested.

The girls had spent yesterday putting up notices around town and knocking on

doors to ask if anyone had lost their
guinea pig. But no one had. So the girls
had named her Coco and Lily's parents
agreed that she could live at the hospital
until they found her owner.

Lily closed the hutch, then listened.
"Did you hear that?" She looked at
Jess in excitement. "It sounded like a
meow . . ."

Jess ran to open the barn door. A
beautiful golden cat bounded inside.

"Goldie!" Lily cried.

Goldie was a magical cat and their
special friend. She lived in Friendship

Forest, a secret world where all the animals could talk!

Lily and Jess bent to pet her. But Goldie didn't seem as happy to see them as she usually was. She wasn't purring and her tail was flicking from side to side.

"My kitten Pixie does that when she's upset," said Jess anxiously. "I wonder what Grizelda's done this time!"

Grizelda was a wicked witch who wanted to make all the animals leave Friendship Forest so she could have it for herself. She had some helpers in her mischief-making—dragons! So far, Lily

and Jess had stopped three of the dragons
from ruining the forest, but they knew
Grizelda still had one more dragon left.

Lily crouched down. "Whatever's
happening, we're ready to help," she told
the cat. "Take us back to Friendship
Forest, Goldie, and then you can tell us
what's wrong!"

Goldie mewed up at them. Then she ran
out of the barn and across the lawn. Lily
and Jess dashed after her, and followed
her over the stepping stones that crossed
Brightley Stream and led up to the
Friendship Tree. Its branches were bare,

but as the cat reached it, buds appeared on every twig and burst into leaves as green as Goldie's eyes. A bumblebee buzzed around the yellow flowers that had sprung up under the tree, and birds chased each other through the branches, singing happily.

Goldie pawed at some words carved into the tree's bark. Together, the girls read them aloud: "Friendship Forest!"

A door appeared in the trunk. Jess grasped the leaf-shaped handle and opened it. Golden light shone out, dancing over them like sunbeams.

Goldie stepped through
the door. With a thrill, Lily and Jess
stooped to follow her. Their skin tingled
like lemonade bubbles as they shrank so
they were a little smaller than usual.

But when the golden light faded, the girls
gave gasps of horror. Friendship Forest was
usually filled with warmth and sunshine,
but today it looked completely different.
The tree branches thrashed around wildly
in a fierce wind and leaves and petals
swirled through the air. Rain poured
down, splashing in puddles everywhere.

"What's happening?" Lily cried, her

dark hair whipping around
her face.

"It's a storm!" cried Goldie over
the howling wind. "I've never seen
one this bad!"

Now that they were in the forest,
Goldie could talk to them at
last. She stood upright beside
the girls, almost up to
their shoulders,
one paw
holding her

glittery scarf so it couldn't be snatched
away by the wind.

As they huddled against the tree trunk,
Jess turned to their friend. "Goldie,"
she cried in alarm, "what's wrong with
Friendship Forest?"

CHAPTER TWO

The Terrible Storm

A flash of lightning streaked across the sky. Immediately, a thunderclap boomed around them, making Lily and Jess jump.

"All the animals must be so scared!" cried Lily. "The storm could blow away their houses!"

Goldie nodded, her whiskers quivering

with worry. She reached behind them into a hollow in the tree's roots and pulled out three hooded capes, made of laurel leaves and magnolia petals stitched together.

"I left them here when I went through the tree to fetch you," Goldie shouted over the storm's roar. "They'll protect us from the wind and rain!"

The girls wrapped themselves in the capes thankfully.

"Did Grizelda cause this storm, Goldie?" asked Jess.

"I think so," the cat said. "Remember what she made the other dragons do?"

The girls could hardly forget. Grizelda had made Chilly the ice dragon stop the Flufftail squirrel family from looking after the Shining House, which made the forest sunny. It had quickly become cold and gloomy. Then the Prickleback hedgehog family were turned to stone by Dusty, the sand dragon, so they couldn't keep the river flowing properly with their waterwheel. Next, Smudge the shadow dragon had turned the Fuzzybrush fox family into shadows, so they couldn't dance to make the stars come out.

"Grizelda's still got one dragon left," Jess said with a groan. "Breezy the storm dragon!"

"I think Grizelda's sent her to the Whirligig," said Goldie.

"What's the Whirligig?" asked Lily.

"It's a magical windmill," Goldie explained. "The Gigglepip guinea pig family live there. They turn the sails of the windmill at exactly the right speed to send a lovely, gentle breeze through Friendship Forest."

A gust of wind howled as it swept around them, tugging at their capes.

"That wasn't a gentle breeze!" Lily cried. "Something must have happened to the Gigglepips!"

"Let's go and find out!" yelled Jess.

They hurried through the forest. The little cottages in Toadstool Glade had their doors and windows tightly shut. Chestnuts were stuffed into chimney tops to stop the rain getting in.

The Longwhiskers rabbit family, who ran the Toadstool Café, were getting soaked as they moved tables, chairs, and sunshades indoors. Through the windows, the girls spotted their friends Emily Prickleback the hedgehog and Lola Velvetnose the mole sheltering inside.

A mouse ran across the glade, clutching a tiny umbrella made of ivy leaves.

"Look! There's little Molly Twinkletail!" cried Lily.

Suddenly, the wind caught the umbrella and whisked the tiny mouse into the air.

"Help!" Molly squealed.

Jess darted
across Toadstool
Glade. She
caught Molly
gently. The
little mouse
sat quivering in
her hand. Jess
kissed her tiny
damp head and
lifted her to the front door of the
Twinkletails' cottage, high up on a tree
branch.

"You're safe now, Molly," she said.

"Make sure your family stays inside until this awful storm is over."

"Thank you, Jess! I will!" cried Molly, as her dad opened the door. She ran inside to a chorus of squeaks and squeals.

"Poor Molly," said Goldie, when Jess ran back to her and Lily. Her tail twitched anxiously. "We'd better hurry. If the storm keeps going, the littlest animals will be swept away, just like Molly was!"

As the girls struggled through a big cloud of leaves being swirled around by the wind, Goldie gasped.

Ahead was a horribly familiar sight.
A yellow-green orb was floating through
the storm toward them!

"Oh, no!" cried Jess and Lily together.

With a *cra-ack*, the orb burst in a
shower of smelly yellow sparks that hissed
as raindrops hit them. In its place stood
Grizelda the witch!

CHAPTER THREE

Gigglepips in Trouble

The witch's cloak flapped in the wind, whipping around her purple tunic and tight black pants. Her green hair waved wildly in the wind, like a nest of snakes.

Grizelda fixed the girls and Goldie with a cold smile. "You interfering girls are too late to stop my plan this time," she said, looking at them down her long nose. "And so is your silly pet cat."

Jess bravely stepped toward her. "Goldie's not our pet, and she's not silly, either!" she cried.

Grizelda just cackled. "I've saved my most powerful dragon for last," she told them. "Ha ha haaa! Thanks to Breezy, this storm will rip every leaf from every tree. All the food growing on the Treasure Tree will be blown to the ground and ruined!"

Jess and Lily looked at each other in dismay. This was awful news. The magical Treasure Tree was where all the forest animals got their food.

Grizelda pranced in delight. "All the animals will have to leave," she screeched, "and the forest will be mine!"

Lily clenched her fists. "We'll stop you, Grizelda!" she yelled.

"You're too late," Grizelda sneered.

"It's never too late!" Jess shouted over the wind's howl.

"We'll stop the storm somehow," Goldie told the witch. "Lily and Jess are clever and brave, and they won't let you win!"

But Grizelda wasn't even listening. She rubbed her bony hands together. "Kidnapping those dragons was the best thing I ever did!" she crowed. Then she snapped her fingers and disappeared in a burst of smelly sparks.

The girls and Goldie stood for a moment, staring at each other miserably.

Goldie said, "Come on. Let's get to the Whirligig. If there's a way to stop the storm, I know you two will find it."

The three friends raced through the forest. They dodged chestnuts, acorns, and twigs as the wind blew them through the air, and skidded over the wet leaves that blew around the ground.

Goldie led them out of the trees to a little hill. On top of it stood a purple-and-yellow-striped windmill with four yellow wooden sails. They were spinning wildly, so fast they were almost a blur.

Goldie gave a gasp. "No wonder the wind is so strong, the sails normally turn slowly and steadily!" she said. "Only the Gigglepips can work the Whirligig and make the storm stop, but I can't see them anywhere!"

But she had barely finished speaking when faint squeaks reached them through the wind and rain.

"Look!" cried Jess, pointing at a nearby tree. "What is that?"

They peered up into the treetop.

A small column of wind was whirling

around on a branch. Through it, they

could just see four tiny, frightened faces.

"It's a tornado," Goldie cried, "with the

Gigglepip family

trapped inside!

How can we get

them down?"

"Shh," said

Lily. She listened

hard, straining

to hear over the

storm.

"Did you
hear that
squeak? It
sounds closer."

"Help!" a small voice
squeaked sadly. "Help me!"

"Over here!" Lily led them to a low,
thin branch. Clinging to it was a tiny
guinea pig. She looked very wobbly and
frightened. Her wet fur was the color of
vanilla ice cream, with caramel patches,

and she was wearing a pretty pink rose on a ribbon around her neck.

Lily gently lifted her down.

"You poor thing," Lily said, cradling the trembling creature in her arms.

"It's Rosie Gigglepip," Goldie said. "It's okay, Rosie. These girls are Jess and Lily, and they've come to help."

Lily wrapped her cape around the shivering guinea pig.

"Thank you," said Rosie, snuggling in.

"Can you tell us what happened?" asked Jess gently.

"It was so scary," Rosie said. "A red

dragon flew down and blew at the
Whirligig so hard that the sails started
turning too fast. Way too fast! My family
tried to slow it down again, but then she
blew at us and we went flying up into the

air! The wind won't stop until me and my family slow the Whirligig down again." Rosie's tiny chin wobbled. "I managed to grab that branch," she said, "but my mom and dad, and my sisters, Posie and Josie, were swept up in that swirly wind. I was so frightened!"

Rosie looked at the girls and Goldie with tear-filled brown eyes. "Please help them!" she begged.

CHAPTER FOUR

The Toadstool Café

"We can't climb up to the Gigglepip family," said Goldie. "There aren't any branches low enough."

"Even if we could reach them," said Lily, "I don't know how we'd get them out of that tornado. It's spinning so fast!"

"We have to do something," said Jess.

"Let's go to the Toadstool Café and try to think of a plan. Maybe some of the animals there will know what we can do."

"Good idea!" said Goldie.

Goldie put her paws to her mouth and shouted up to where the Gigglepip family were trapped inside the tornado. "It's all right! Rosie's safe and warm, and we'll find a way to save you soon!"

"Thank you!" A squeaky voice called down through the wind and the rain.

"Don't worry about us," squeaked another Gigglepip, "we're okay, we're just a little dizzy!"

Lily tucked Rosie inside her cape and they hurried back to Toadstool Glade, dodging swaying branches and the swirls of leaves being tossed around. Just as the Toadstool Café's spotty roof came into sight, there was a roar that bellowed over the sound of the wind.

Lily spun around and gave a cry. "Oh, no! Breezy's here!"

The dragon flew overhead, right toward them. She was almost as big as the girls and her red scales glittered in the rain. She playfully swiped some leaves that were being blown around, then opened her mouth.

"Run!" cried Goldie.

They dodged behind a tree trunk just as Breezy blew.

Whoooooooooooooooooooooooooh!

"Hold on!" cried Goldie.

They hid behind the tree as Breezy's
powerful blast of wind shot past them. It
was so strong that it lifted poor Rosie up
into the air. She gave a terrified squeak.
Lily reached and caught hold of her paw
just in time, but then she felt her own feet
being lifted off the ground, too!

"We're being blown away!" Lily cried.

"I'll catch you!" yelled Jess. "Goldie, hold on to me!"

Jess wrapped her arms around the tree trunk and Goldie grabbed on to her. Lily reached out her hand and held on to Goldie. Her other hand was still tightly holding on to Rosie's tiny paw. The four friends held each other tight. If they let go, they would be swept away!

At last, the blast of wind died down. Lily's feet touched back onto the ground and she cuddled Rosie.

"Thank you!" squeaked the little guinea pig in a shaky voice.

"Thank goodness we're all okay," panted Jess.

But Goldie's eyes were wide with horror. Lily and Jess turned around and looked at the Toadstool Café in amazement. Breezy's blast of air had blown the café's roof right off!

Lily, Jess, and Goldie peered inside the café. Emily Prickleback was staring in shocked surprise as rain sloshed into her honey milk shake. Mrs. Longwhiskers tried to protect a tray of cakes from the storm with her apron. Puddles were

already gathering on the wooden

floor.

Mr. Longwhiskers looked sadly at

his ruined café. "Those dragons are

ruining everything in our forest," he said.
"What can we do?"

Jess groaned as Breezy swooped over
Toadstool Glade again. She put her hands
on her hips. "Look what you've done,
Breezy!" she shouted up at her.

Breezy just giggled and aimed another
blast of wind at a tree. All the leaves flew
off and swirled around them.

Rosie gave a sob. "I . . . I . . . I want my
mommy!"

The wind seemed to carry her words
up to Breezy. The dragon suddenly looked
upset and landed with a thump beside

them. "I miss *my* mommy, too," she said miserably.

Lily, Jess, and Goldie stared at her in surprise. "Breezy, are you a grown-up dragon?" Lily asked.

Breezy shook her head. "Of course not!" she said. "I'm only little, so my storms aren't big enough for Grizelda. She wants me to make storms as big as my mommy's."

The girls and Goldie looked at each other in amazement. The dragons were only babies!

"There are dragons bigger than Breezy?" said Rosie, her eyes very wide.

"It sounds like it," said Jess. "Breezy's mom must be huge!"

An idea was starting to come to Lily. "What about Chilly, Dusty, and Smudge?" she asked. "Are they babies, too?"

"They're my brothers and my sister," explained Breezy. "We all miss Mommy." She sighed, letting out a puff of air that made the girls' hair blow back and ruffled Goldie's and Rosie's fur.

"Your mommy must miss you, too," Jess
told Breezy. "Why don't you go home?"

The dragon shook her scaly head.
"Can't! Grizelda put a spell on us. We
can't fly away from the forest."

Goldie turned to the others, her tail
twitching crossly. "Grizelda said she
kidnapped the dragons, didn't she? They
don't want to be here at all!"

"I know they've caused lots of problems,
but I feel sorry for them," said Jess.

Lily nodded. "If we can break Grizelda's
spell, I bet they'd go home!"

46

CHAPTER FIVE

Searching for Spells

When they told Breezy their idea, the dragon shook her scaly head. "No one can stop Grizelda's magic," she said sadly. "We're stuck here forever."

"Well, we're going to try," Jess told her, pushing her windswept curls out of her face. "But first, will you do something for us? Can you free the Gigglepips from the tornado?"

Rosie's little face peeked out from inside Lily's cape. "Oh, yes!" she squeaked, clasping her paws together. "Please, Breezy!"

But Breezy shook her head sadly. "I only know how to start tornados," she said. "Mommy hasn't shown me how to stop them yet."

Rosie's whiskers drooped with disappointment.

"It's okay," Lily said, cuddling her close. "We'll free them soon, I promise.

Now, where can we find out about dragons and dragon magic?"

They all thought hard as the wind swirled around them. Then Rosie gave an excited squeak.

"I know!" said the little guinea pig. "Mrs. Taptree's library!"

"Of course!" cried Jess. "Let's go!"

They hurried through the raging storm, struggling over broken branches and weaving through great billowing clouds of fallen leaves. Only Breezy seemed to find the journey easy, zipping along above them. At last, Goldie stopped at a broad chestnut tree. Its branches were swaying wildly in the storm and it had a door in its trunk. "Here we are!"

Mrs. Taptree's chicks, Dig and Tipper, were peering through the window. They waved excitedly and their mother opened the door.

"Come in out of the wind!" Mrs. Taptree cried. "Quick! Quick!" Then she caught sight of Breezy, and squawked, "No, no! You'll blow away my books!"

"Breezy will wait outside, Mrs. Taptree," said Goldie. She hurriedly explained to the Taptrees why they'd come. "Do you have any books on dragons?"

"Ladders?" said Mrs. Taptree, clapping her wings together. "Dragon books, please! Quick!"

The ladders glided along the shelves. Goldie and the girls collected some books and searched through the pages as fast as they could.

Mrs. Taptree closed a book. "This tells you how to clean dragons' teeth," she said. "That's no good."

"I've got *How to Dance Like a Dragon*," said Lily.

"Mine's about teaching dragons to swim," Jess said.

Goldie shut her book. "This is about famous dragons and their daring deeds," she said.

But Rosie gave another excited squeak. "Look!" she cried. "I've found a spell to summon dragons!"

Jess glanced outside at the wild storm.

"I think there are already too many dragons in Friendship Forest, Rosie. We don't need any more!"

Rosie frowned thoughtfully. "No, wait," she said. "Grizelda's spell stops the dragons flying away from the forest . . . but maybe we could summon their mother to come and get them!"

Goldie's green eyes gleamed. "That's a wonderful idea! Oh, good job, Rosie!"

"And Breezy said her mom could stop the tornado, didn't she?" added Lily. "So if we can do the spell, we can ask her to free the Gigglepips!"

Rosie gave a delighted squeak and
clapped her paws together.

Jess studied the book. "Smoke Signal
Summoning Spell," she read. "To summon
a dragon, you must send clouds of smoke
up into the air. It's important to follow a
special pattern:
Smoke . . .

smoke smoke . . .

smoke . . . smoke

smoke . . ." She

pulled out the

little sketchbook

and pencil she

always kept in her pocket, and copied
down the pattern.

"There's just one problem," Lily said.
"Where can we get smoke in the middle
of a storm? It's too wet to make a fire."

The little guinea pig squeaked again. "I
know where to get smoke!"

"Where?" everyone cried.

Rosie smiled. "From the dragons, of
course!"

CHAPTER SIX

Gathering Dragons

"Good luck!" called Mrs. Taptree, as the three friends and Rosie stepped back out into the storm.

"Breezy!" Goldie shouted over the noise of the wind. "Breezy, we're ready to try breaking Grizelda's spell!"

The red dragon gave an excited twirl in the air as she flew over.

"Yippee!" she cried. "I'm going to see Mommy soon!"

Jess laughed. "That's the plan. Grizelda's magic won't let you fly away from the forest, so we're going to summon your mom here to take you home. What do you think?"

Breezy gave a roar of delight and blew a gust of wind so strong it made a tall beech tree shudder.

"To call your mom, we just need you to breathe your fire so we can have some smoke," Goldie explained.

But Breezy's face fell. "Fire?" she said. "Smoke?" She shook her scaly head. "I'm no good at breathing fire. My brothers and sister are much better than me, and I don't know where they are."

From inside Lily's cape, Rosie gave a sob. "That means I won't see my mommy either! Or my daddy, or my sisters Posie and Josie . . ."

"Hang on," Jess said. "We've helped all the other dragons—Chilly and Dusty and Smudge—we know where they are!"

Breezy flew a loop-the-loop. "They can make smoke!" she said excitedly.

Goldie grinned at the girls. "Then let's gather some dragons!"

They set off through the storm. Rosie curled around Lily's neck and peeped out of the cape hood.

"There!" Goldie shouted over the wind, pointing to a soft light up ahead. "The glowworm bush—that means we've reached the Winter Cave!"

"Chilly's inside," Lily told Breezy. "Can you call him for us?"

The red dragon flew down, skidding to a stop by the cave entrance. She stuck her nose inside. "Chilly, come with me!" she rumbled. "The girls and Goldie are going to fetch Mommy!"

Chilly came out from the cave, his eyes wide. "Will we really see Mommy again?" he asked.

"We hope so," Jess said.

"Yippee!" shouted Chilly and blew a puff of snow into the air.

"To Coral Cove next!" said Goldie.

Dusty the yellow dragon loved sunbathing, so Lily and Jess had told her about Coral Cove, a little beach by the river. It was near Grizelda's dark, gloomy tower, so they kept well hidden in the wind-tossed bushes as Breezy told Dusty what was happening.

Then they hurried through the storm to the lighthouse where the Fuzzybrush fox family lived. Smudge the black dragon had loved dancing with Ruby Fuzzybrush, Goldie, and the girls so much that little Ruby had asked him to stay with them.

When Smudge came out to join his

brother and sisters, all the Fuzzybrushes
stood at the door, waving.

"Good-bye, Smudge!" Ruby called
over the wind that whistled around the
lighthouse. "Remember the dance moves I
showed you!"

"I will!" Smudge promised. He did a
twirl in the air, but a gust caught his tail
and he bumped into one of the swaying

trees,
scattering
soot everywhere.
Lily giggled. "He's
still as clumsy as ever!"
Jess looked up at the four dragons
flying above them and grinned.
"Back to the Whirligig!" she cried.
The girls and Goldie huddled
under their capes as
they battled
their way back
through the
trees.

Lily kept Rosie inside her cape, safely tucked under one arm. By the time they reached the magical windmill, the dragons were very excited.

Goldie called up to the Gigglepips, who were still trapped up inside the whirling tornado. "Don't be frightened of the dragons," she shouted, "they're here to help rescue you!"

The four baby dragons landed on the wet ground.

Jess took out her notebook, where she'd written down the smoke-signal pattern. "We need you all to blow big puffs of smoke together," she told Chilly, Dusty, and Smudge. "I'll tell you when. And Breezy, we need your wind to blow the smoke straight up. Remember, we don't want any fire, just smoke!"

Dusty looked disappointed. "Not even a little bit of fire?"

Jess shook her head.

"A really tiny bit?" begged Smudge.

"Definitely not," said Lily firmly.

The dragons sighed.

"Everyone ready?" asked Jess. "One . . . two . . . three . . . BLOW!"

CHAPTER SEVEN

Smoke Signals

Chilly, Dusty, and Smudge all puffed out
their cheeks and blew. Jets of smoke shot
out of their mouths, forming a huge, dark
cloud above them. Then Breezy's wind
caught it and the smoke whirled up,
higher and higher in the sky.

"BLOW, BLOW!" Jess shouted.

The dragons puffed out two
more clouds of smoke, one following
quickly after the other. After a moment,
Jess yelled, "BLOW!" Then she shouted,
"BLOW! BLOW!" again.

The clouds of smoke rose up high
above the forest.

"Well done,

everyone!" cried Goldie.

The dragons flapped their wings

happily. Breezy did a loop-the-loop and

landed next to her brothers and sister.

Jess grinned. "Now we've just got to

wait for their mom to arrive."

They all stood looking up at the sky.

The wind howled around them, making

Jess and Lily's capes flap. Rosie stood

under the tree where her family were

69

trapped, her little paws tightly crossed for good luck.

But nothing happened.

Breezy gave a huge sigh that rippled the tops of the trees. "It didn't work," she said sadly. "Mommy isn't coming!"

The four baby dragons huddled together miserably.

"I don't understand," said Lily, shaking her head with dismay. "What did we do wrong?"

"I don't know," said Jess. "But the dragons are still stuck in the forest, and we've got no way of getting the poor Gigglepip family down."

Rosie stood by herself, looking wet and forlorn.

Suddenly, Lily's eye was caught by something flying toward them through the rain. She grabbed Jess's arm.

"Look, it did work! She's coming!" Then she gasped. "Oh, no—that's not a dragon . . . it's Grizelda!"

The witch's yellow-green orb floated toward them. As it exploded into stinking yellow sparks, the baby dragons dived

under a tree, their wings wrapped around
each other.

The sparks cleared, revealing the witch.
The wind blew her green hair around her
head even more than usual, and her thin,
bony face was purple with rage.

"I might have guessed!" Grizelda

screeched. "So you
pesky girls made those
smoke signals! What
were you doing?"

Before anyone could
reply, Grizelda spotted
the dragons. She pointed

at them,
sending a jet
of hot sparks
that made them
jump.

"What are you doing here?" she snapped. "Go and wait in the dungeon beneath my tower. Now!"

But then a great dark shadow fell over them all.

Lily and Jess looked up.

A huge dragon was hovering above the clearing. Her scales were all the colors of her babies—red, yellow, blue, and black—and she was even bigger than the Toadstool Café.

The girls grasped each other's hands.

"Our spell worked after all!" Jess cried. "We've summoned the dragons' mom!"

Lily's eyes were wide. "Jess, do you think we did the right thing? I bet she could burn the whole forest down with one breath if she wanted to!"

"I don't know," said Jess, "but we're about to find out . . ."

The mother dragon swooped down and landed neatly beside the Whirligig.

"Mommy! Mommy!" yelled the dragons.

They flapped over to her, and their
mother folded her wings around them.

"My beautiful babies," the mother
dragon said in a deep, soft voice. "I'm so
happy to see you!"

And she planted a kiss on each of their
heads. The baby dragons gave gurgling
roars of delight and snuggled even closer
under her wings.

Jess grinned at Lily. "We definitely did the right thing!"

"I've been so worried," the mother dragon said. "Where have you been?"

From the corner of her eye, Lily caught sight of Grizelda tiptoeing away toward the trees.

"I'd forgotten she was there," Lily whispered to her friend.

"Chilly hasn't," Jess giggled. The blue dragon was pointing his wing at Grizelda.

"We were kidnapped," he told his mother. "Kidnapped by her!"

Breezy, Smudge, and Dusty flapped

over to Grizelda. "Her! It was her!" they cried.

The mother's eyes flashed silver. "Bad!" she thundered. She reared up. With a roar that was far louder than the storm, she blew a stream of red, blue, yellow, black, and ice-white flames at the witch.

Grizelda jumped out of the way just in time. She tumbled into a pool of mud and landed with her legs in the air.

"If you come near my babies again," the mother dragon roared, "I'll toast you to a crisp!"

Grizelda scrambled upright. "I'm sorry!" she screeched, staggering as her high heels sank in the mud. Her green hair, covered in brown ooze, stuck to her bony cheeks. "I'm sorry! I'm going!"

With a snap of her fingers, she disappeared in a splatter of smelly sparks.

Everyone cheered. The dragons flew happily around their mother and Lily picked up Rosie and spun her around. The little guinea pig squeaked happily.

"We've defeated Grizelda!" Jess cried.

"Friendship Forest is safe!" Lily chanted.

They grabbed Goldie's paws and danced around each other, not caring about the storm.

The young dragons flapped happily above them, while the mother dragon looked down at the girls.

"I am Saffire," she said. "Thank you for your kindness to my little ones, and for bringing me here. What are your names?"

"I'm Jess, and this is Lily," said Jess. "Our friends are Rosie Gigglepip and Goldie. They live here."

Saffire looked at the trees whipping around in the wind, the snapped branches, and the fallen leaves. "Breezy!" she bellowed. "Did you make this mess?"

Breezy nodded sheepishly.

Saffire turned to her other babies. "And I suppose you've been spoiling this lovely forest, too?"

The young dragons hung their heads.

"Sort of," said Dusty.

"A little bit," said Chilly.

"Well, maybe a lot," admitted Smudge.

"Naughty children!" said Saffire. "If

you made the mess, you must clean it up.
We're not going
home until
you do."

Rosie
bravely
crept forward
and tapped Saffire's huge clawed foot.
"Please, do you think you could help my
family?" She pointed up to the tornado
in the tree. "They've been trapped there
for a long time, and Breezy said that you
could free them. Then we can fix the
Whirligig and stop the storm!"

Saffire's great head swooped down until her big, scaly nose almost touched little Rosie's pink one.

"Of course I'll help, little one," the mother dragon said.

CHAPTER EIGHT

Surprises

Saffire strode up to the tree where the Gigglepips were trapped. She opened her huge mouth, but instead of a roar, she let out a stream of bubbles. They floated around the tornado, and as they burst in a shimmer of sparkles, the whirling wind vanished. In a flash Mr. and

 83

Mrs. Gigglepip, Josie, and Posie were standing safely on a branch, free at last.

Rosie squealed with delight. "Thank you!" she cried.

Saffire dipped her nose toward the guinea pigs. "Climb on," she said with a smile.

The four Gigglepips hopped onto the dragon's nose, and she carefully lowered them to where Rosie was waiting.

"We're so happy to see you!" cried Mr. Gigglepip.

"Thank you so much for looking after Rosie!" said Mrs. Gigglepip.

"And for saving us!" squeaked Posie and Josie.

"It's about time we stopped this terrible storm," said Mr. Gigglepip. "Come on— let's fix the Whirligig. Everyone inside and hold tight to a whirler!"

Jess and Lily peeped through the doorway and watched each guinea pig take hold of a whirler, which was like a spinning top. Some whirlers were big and

some small, and the Gigglepips darted
from one to the other, spinning them,
stopping them, then spinning again.

"That's complicated!" said Jess. "No
wonder only the Gigglepips can take care
of the Whirligig."

The sails began to slow down. As
they did so, the wind began to drop. "It's
working!" cried Lily.

The rain stopped, the sun came out,
and a rainbow arched across the sky. A
soft breeze blew gently through the trees.

"Finally! The storm's over!" said Jess happily, shaking out her tangled curls while Lily shrugged off her cape.

"Look," cried Goldie. "All the animals are coming out!"

A family of blue birds flapped their wings dry and turned their faces to the sun. Lola Velvetnose strolled over, whistling cheerfully. Lily and Jess waved as the Prickleback family gathered around the Whirligig, drying off their spines. "Sunshine at last!" called Mrs. Prickleback. "Now, what can we do to help clean up?"

Before long, all the forest creatures

were busy cleaning up the mess made by the storm. The young dragons flew back and forth, taking fallen branches to Mr. Cleverfeather, the owl, for him to use in his inventions. Saffire breathed warm air into the Toadstool Café to dry it out, then lifted the roof and put it back on.

As dusk fell, the forest was almost back to normal.

Mr. Longwhiskers hopped onto a tree stump. "Everyone's invited to a celebration at the Toadstool Café," he shouted. "And the dragons will be our special guests!"

Soon the girls, Goldie, the Gigglepips,

the four baby dragons, and all the animals
were sitting around tables outside the
Toadstool Café. Saffire sat nearby,
looking proud and happy.

"My children were very naughty," the
dragon said, "but Jess, Lily, and Goldie
understood that Grizelda made them
behave like that. To say thank you, I
have a gift for you all. Look!"

She breathed a long stream of sparks
of every color imaginable, up into the
darkening sky.

The animals watched, amazed, as the
sparks formed into whirling, spinning,

shooting patterns, filling the night
with glittering, sparkling light.

"Wow!" said Jess.

"It's the best firework display ever!"
cried Lily.

When it was over, Saffire said, "Now
I must take my little ones home."

The young dragons clung to her,
looking upset.

"But Grizelda's spell means we can't
fly out of the forest," said Smudge
anxiously.

Saffire smiled. "Climb onto my back,"

she said, stretching out her rainbow-colored wings. "No spell can stop *me* flying!"

Moments later, the dragon family soared into the sky, calling, "Bye, Lily and Jess! Bye, Goldie!"

Once they were out of sight, Lily sighed. "I guess it's time for us to go home, too."

She and Jess hugged Rosie, the Gigglepips, and all their other friends. Then, waving good-bye, they followed Goldie through the trees.

"The forest looks lovely again," said

Jess. The last raindrops were glittering like diamonds on a starflower bush.

"And look, the Friendship Tree's golden leaves are as beautiful as ever," said Lily, as they arrived.

Goldie took their hands in her paws. "The forest is safe thanks to you!"

Jess and Lily exchanged glances.

"Grizelda will probably come up with a horrible new plan," said Lily.

"But we'll be ready to stop her," added Jess firmly.

Goldie smiled. "I know you will."

She touched a paw to the tree trunk, and a door appeared.

The girls hugged her, then stepped inside, into the shimmering light.

When the golden glow disappeared, Jess and Lily found themselves back in Brightley Meadow.

"What an adventure!" said Jess, as they walked back to Helping Paw.

"It was amazing!" Lily said with a grin. They went into the barn and peeped into Coco's hutch. The guinea pig was asleep in her nest of sweet-smelling hay.

But there was something else there, too, nestling beside her.

"She had a baby!" whispered Lily.

Jess grinned. "So *that's* why she wasn't feeling right!"

The tiny creature was a little smaller than Lily's hand, and had golden-brown fur. She blinked up at the girls.

"She's so pretty!" said Lily.

Just then, Mr. and Mrs. Hart came into the barn, too.

"Mom! Dad!" said Lily. "Guess what? Coco had a baby!"

Mr. and Mrs. Hart just smiled.

Lily gasped. "You knew!"

"We wanted it to be a surprise," said
Mr. Hart, with a grin.

"Jess has her kitten, Pixie," said
Mrs. Hart, "so we thought it would be
nice for you to have a pet, too. Would
you like to keep the baby?" she asked.
"And Coco, too, of course, if no one
claims her."

Lily hugged her parents. "Yes, please!
Thank you!" she said happily.

Jess was thrilled for her. "What will
you call the baby?"

Lily looked at the tiny creature. "Her

fur's lovely and golden," she said, "so I think I'll call her Honey—Honey Rose!"

Jess grinned. "Perfect!"

As Mr. and Mrs. Hart started cleaning out the other hutches, Coco woke up and nuzzled Honey.

Lily laughed. "She's such a good mom, just like Saffire!"

"I hope Goldie visits us again soon," Jess said.

"Me, too," Lily agreed.

They shared a smile. They couldn't wait for their next adventure in Friendship Forest!

The End

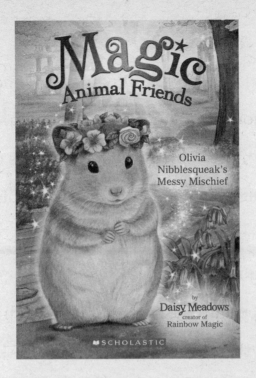

When Jess and Lily return to Friendship Forest, Grizelda casts a spell to make little Olivia Nibblesqueak the hamster think she's a messy creature—just like Grizelda's new helpers! Can Jess and Lily find a way to make Olivia herself again?

Turn the page for a sneak peek of

Olivia Nibblesqueak's Messy Mischief

"Percy Littlepaw!" Olivia said. "That was your third bag! Never mind, you can share mine." She turned to the girls and whispered, "Percy's my best friend. He loves icing so much, I think he must be eating it all!"

Percy started scampering off with the icing, then gave a shout. "Look out!"

Splat!

The new sign above the door was smeared with splattered cake!

"Who did that?" wondered Olivia, turning around.

"Heeheehee!"

Jess looked around, but couldn't see where the giggling came from, then . . .

Splat!

"Hey!" cried Percy as a cake hit him right in the face!

Percy wiped pink icing from his cheek and giggled as he licked his paw clean. But then the animals shrieked and scattered as more cakes zoomed over. *Splat, splat, splat!*

The flying cake covered everything with bits of sponge and icing.

Jess and Lily glanced at each other in amazement. Someone was throwing cakes! But who?

Puzzle Fun!

Can you help Rosie follow the right path to find her rose ribbon?

A)

B)

C)

Lily and Jess love lots of different animals—
both in Friendship Forest
and in the real world.

Here are their top facts about

GUINEA PIGS

like Rosie Gigglepip.

- Guinea pigs are sometimes called "cavies" and come from the grasslands and lower slopes of the Andes Mountains in South America.

- Guinea pigs are very active. They are awake for up to 20 hours a day and only sleep for short times.

- Guinea pigs' teeth grow all the time. Eating lots of hay and grass helps wear their teeth down so they don't get too long.

- Guinea pigs are group animals and have close families with up to ten members.

- Guinea pigs love to be held and they will make purring noises when they are happy.

RAINBOW magic™

Which Magical Fairies Have You Met?

- ☐ The Rainbow Fairies
- ☐ The Weather Fairies
- ☐ The Jewel Fairies
- ☐ The Pet Fairies
- ☐ The Dance Fairies
- ☐ The Music Fairies
- ☐ The Sports Fairies
- ☐ The Party Fairies
- ☐ The Ocean Fairies
- ☐ The Night Fairies
- ☐ The Magical Animal Fairies
- ☐ The Princess Fairies
- ☐ The Superstar Fairies
- ☐ The Fashion Fairies
- ☐ The Sugar & Spice Fairies
- ☐ The Earth Fairies
- ☐ The Magical Crafts Fairies
- ☐ The Baby Animal Rescue Fairies
- ☐ The Fairy Tale Fairies

◼ SCHOLASTIC

Find all of your favorite fairy friends at
scholastic.com/rainbowmagic

RMFAIRY13

SPECIAL EDITION

Which Magical Fairies Have You Met?

- ❑ Joy the Summer Vacation Fairy
- ❑ Holly the Christmas Fairy
- ❑ Kylie the Carnival Fairy
- ❑ Stella the Star Fairy
- ❑ Shannon the Ocean Fairy
- ❑ Trixie the Halloween Fairy
- ❑ Gabriella the Snow Kingdom Fairy
- ❑ Juliet the Valentine Fairy
- ❑ Mia the Bridesmaid Fairy
- ❑ Flora the Dress-Up Fairy
- ❑ Paige the Christmas Play Fairy
- ❑ Emma the Easter Fairy
- ❑ Cara the Camp Fairy
- ❑ Destiny the Rock Star Fairy
- ❑ Belle the Birthday Fairy

- ❑ Olympia the Games Fairy
- ❑ Selena the Sleepover Fairy
- ❑ Cheryl the Christmas Tree Fairy
- ❑ Florence the Friendship Fairy
- ❑ Lindsay the Luck Fairy
- ❑ Brianna the Tooth Fairy
- ❑ Autumn the Falling Leaves Fairy
- ❑ Keira the Movie Star Fairy
- ❑ Addison the April Fool's Day Fairy
- ❑ Bailey the Babysitter Fairy
- ❑ Natalie the Christmas Stocking Fairy
- ❑ Lila and Myla the Twins Fairies
- ❑ Chelsea the Congratulations Fairy
- ❑ Carly the School Fairy
- ❑ Angelica the Angel Fairy
- ❑ Blossom the Flower Girl Fairy

■SCHOLASTIC

Find all of your favorite fairy friends at
scholastic.com/rainbowmagic

3 stories in each one!

HiT entertainment

RMSPECIAL17

Visit Friendship Forest, where animals can talk and magic exists!

Meet best friends Jess and Lily and their adorable animal pals in this enchanting series from the creator of Rainbow Magic!

SCHOLASTIC
scholastic.com

MAGICAF2